ANIMAL ARK

Llama on the Loose

Lucy Daniels

With special thanks to Sarah Shillam

For Hannah

Illustrations by Jo Anne Davies for Artful Doodlers

ORCHARD BOOKS

First published in Great Britain in 2019 by The Watts Publishing Group

1 3 5 7 9 10 8 6 4 2

Text copyright © Working Partners, 2019
Illustrations copyright © Working Partners, 2019

A CIP catalogue record for this book
is available from the British Library.

ISBN 978 1 40835 923 5

Printed and bound in Great Britain by Clays Ltd, Elcograf S.p.A

The paper and board used in this book are made from wood from responsible sources.

Orchard Books
An imprint of
Hachette Children's Group
Part of The Watts Publishing Group Limited
Carmelite House
50 Victoria Embankment
London EC4Y 0DZ

An Hachette UK Company
www.hachette.co.uk
www.hachettechildrens.co.uk

CONTENTS

CHAPTER ONE

"Look, Sam, I can see Lliam! Or is that Llarry?" Amelia Haywood peered through the car window at a pair of long white llama ears sticking up behind the hedge. She had been best friends with Sam since she had moved to Welford Village and they had started helping out at Animal Ark, the local veterinary surgery. That morning they were travelling with the vets, Mr and Mrs Hope, to check up on the animals at the Parish family's petting farm before school.

"It's probably Lliam," said Sam, leaning over her shoulder. "He likes that corner of the field."

As they drew closer to the petting farm, Amelia heard the bleating of goats and clucking of chickens and she broke into a wide smile.

"How do you know it's not the new llama?" Mr Hope asked from the front passenger seat. He turned to peer at

Amelia and Sam over his glasses.

"Caleb said Llucinda's brown," Sam explained. Their friend Caleb had been talking all week about the new llama his family had adopted.

"I can't wait to meet her!" said Amelia, excitement swelling in her chest.

Mrs Hope smiled at Amelia through the rear-view mirror, her green eyes twinkling, as she pulled into the farmhouse driveway.

The Hopes really understand why I love animals … because they love them too! thought Amelia.

Caleb leapt off the farmhouse porch as Amelia got out of the car. He jogged down the gravel pathway towards them. "Come and see Llucinda! She's so cute!"

Amelia glanced back at the Hopes, who were rummaging in the boot of their car. She and Sam had come along to help them, really.

Mr Hope lifted out his black case, full of medicines and paperwork. "You two go on and meet the new llama," he said.

"The goats won't take long, and we can manage the chickens and pigs quite easily. We'll save the llamas for last!"

Amelia grinned at Sam, and they both broke into a run, following Caleb up the drive. He led them down the side of the house and through the petting farm.

"Hello, Puff and Cookie!" Amelia called out to a pair of guinea pigs, their

twitching noses poking out from a pile of hay.

"Morning, Daisy and Pip!" Sam said, waving at two pigs snuffling in their trough as he ran past their enclosure. Pip looked up and his mouth dropped open, spilling out the corn he'd been chewing. Daisy snorted, a little indignantly. The pigs clearly weren't used to having an audience at breakfast time!

"Here we are!" Caleb called out, as they ran around the back of the goat enclosure and came out by the llamas' field.

A pair of white llamas were jostling each other by the trough, while Mrs

Parish filled it with water. Llarry was
trying to drink straight from the jet that
spurted from the hose. Lliam nudged
Llarry out of the way so he could have a
go too, but he knocked the hose and the
spray went all over Mrs Parish's face!

"Steady on, boys!" she complained,
reaching for a small towel draped over
the fence. "I already showered this
morning, thank you very much!" Lliam

lifted his head up, his eyes level with
hers. "That's better," Mrs Parish told him.
"You two are boisterous today!"

"Where's Llucinda?" asked Amelia. She
couldn't see a third llama anywhere.

Then a furry brown head poked up

above the fence
a little further
along.

"Oh!" Amelia's
breath caught in
her throat. "She's
beautiful!"

Llucinda
flicked her ears
forward and

trotted towards them. She was smaller
than Llarry and Lliam, with long-lashed
chocolate-brown eyes, and she had a
colourful blanket on her back.

Sam stretched out to stroke Llucinda,
but she stepped back and tossed her head.
She opened her mouth …

PTUHHH!

A shower of
spit flew from her
mouth, splattering
Sam's shoulder.

"Yikes!" Sam
froze, his eyes
bulging. Then he
burst out laughing.

Amelia couldn't help laughing too, and she heard Caleb chuckling beside her. The look on Sam's face had been so funny!

Llucinda didn't look amused, though. She backed away from the fence, eyes wide and tongue lolling.

"Here, Sam!" Mrs Parish handed him the towel she'd used earlier, just as Mr and Mrs Hope arrived.

"That's not a good sign, I'm afraid!" said Mrs Hope, wincing. "Llamas in the wild spit at each other to show how important they are."

Mr Hope ruffled Sam's hair. "Llucinda thinks you're the least important llama in

the herd, Sam!"

Mrs Hope opened up the black case and took out a set of needles for the llamas' annual vaccinations, while Mr Hope filled out some paperwork.

"Does Llucinda like her new home?" Amelia asked Mrs Parish.

Mrs Parish frowned. "She's having a bit of trouble settling in."

Amelia reached out, a little hesitantly, bracing herself in case the llama spat at her face

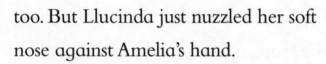

too. But Llucinda just nuzzled her soft nose against Amelia's hand.

"She likes you!" Mrs Parish looked relieved. "Of course, the real test will be tomorrow, when the farm is open to the public."

"Where did she come from?" asked Amelia. She ran a hand down Llucinda's thick, fluffy coat.

"She lived with a family in a village on the other side of Walton," Caleb explained. "But they moved to a house in York with a small garden and there's no space for her there."

"I'm glad she's got a new home," said Amelia. "Even if she did spit at Sam!"

Mrs Hope climbed over the fence and started towards Lliam, who tossed his head and took a step back. She stroked him gently before swiftly administering the injection, just beneath his shoulder blade. Lliam snorted. "I know it's horrible," Mrs Hope said, patting his neck. "At least it's only once a year."

Sam went over to Lliam to soothe him. Mrs Hope turned to Llarry, but he ducked to the side and raced off in a circle around the field. Amelia perched on the fence, ready to look after him once he'd had his injection.

"You're lively today, Llarry!" Mrs Hope said, holding the needle behind her back as she approached.

"We're thinking about starting some llama walking tours, aren't we, Caleb?" Mrs Parish said. "That might burn off some of his energy!"

Caleb nodded, grinning. "There was a

programme about llama trekking on TV last night. It looked really cool!"

"Were people riding the llamas?" asked Sam.

"No, just walking alongside them," explained Caleb.

"Can we help?" Amelia asked, crossing her fingers hopefully.

"That would be great!" Mrs Parish rolled the hosepipe up, and leaned it against a barn wall. "We thought we'd trial our first trek on Sunday."

Sam's face fell. "Oh ... You'll be with your dad then, won't you, Amelia?"

Amelia shook her head. "No – Dad's going to Italy for work. I'll be here in

Welford!" Amelia lived with her mum and gran in Welford, and she usually loved visiting her dad in York every other weekend. But she was glad she wasn't going away this particular weekend.

I wouldn't want to miss this!

"Perfect!" said Caleb. "Come round tomorrow morning and we'll plan our route!"

Mrs Hope gave Llarry his injection and
the llama trotted over to Llucinda, closely
followed by Lliam. The boy llamas both
tried to nudge her into joining them in
a run around the field, but she snorted at
them and made her way back towards
Amelia.

As she reached out to stroke Llucinda,
Amelia's stomach fluttered with
excitement. *A weekend full of llamas!
I can't wait!*

CHAPTER TWO

"Last lesson was fun," said Sam, as he and Amelia walked home after school that day. They were taking a shortcut across a field, and the sun was shining. "Caleb made me laugh when he told Miss Hafiz that volcanos spout llamas instead of lava!"

"He's got llamas on the brain!" said Amelia, climbing over a stile and dropping down on the other side. "Actually, I think I might have, too. They're adorable!"

They approached the wilderness, a patch of land just off the road. When Amelia and Sam had discovered it, it had been wasteland, full of rubbish, but they had cleaned it up and now wildlife could live there safely.

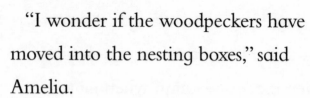

"I wonder if the woodpeckers have moved into the nesting boxes," said Amelia.

"Let's see!" said Sam.

They crossed the road and Amelia

started to pick her way through the grass,
stopping when she heard Sam gasp. She
turned and saw him staring at a sign
fixed to a lamppost, a hand pressed to his
mouth. Amelia hurried over and peered
at it.

COUNCIL NOTICE
A new car park
will be built on
this site.
Work starting
soon.

Cold horror crept through Amelia.
"They can't!"

Sam shook his head. "I don't
understand. Why would anyone want to

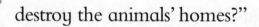

destroy the animals' homes?"

A bit later, in the kitchen of the Old
Mill B&B, where Sam's family lived,
Amelia and Sam ate a quick slice of
toast while Sam's Westie pup Mac
snuffled at his food bowl.

"In a rush?" asked Sam's mum, as she
came in from the sitting room.

"We've made a petition!" said Sam.
"Like those kids we saw on the TV last
week. The ones who were trying to save
the wetlands reserve."

"We're going to ask people to sign it
to object to the new car park," added
Amelia. "They're planning to build it
over the wilderness."

"What a good idea," said Sam's mum.

They put on their shoes at the front door, and Sam collected a pile of papers, each one headed: *SOS – Save Our Sanctuary!* They'd made the petition as soon as they had got in, using the computer and printer on the B&B's reception desk.

"If we get enough signatures, maybe we can persuade the council to build it somewhere else," Amelia said.

Sam's mum looked thoughtful. "Why don't I take one?" she said. "I'll see if my friends will sign it."

Amelia and Sam hurried out with Mac on to the high street, asking passers-by to

sign the petition. While Sam approached
a queue of people waiting to buy ice
creams from a van, Amelia spotted
Dervla, one of Gran's friends, chatting
to another woman. She went over and
explained what the petition was for.

"Of course I'll sign it!" Dervla took
Amelia's pen and added her name. She
turned to her friend. "You'll sign it too,
Jess, won't you?"

Jess shook her head. "I'm sorry, dear,

but we really do need another car park in Welford. Otherwise people park on the pavements, and it's dangerous!"

Amelia met Sam as he walked away from the ice cream queue and told him what Jess had said. "A couple of people complained to me about parking too," Sam replied sadly as they wandered up the road together. "We've only got eight signatures. That's not nearly enough."

"But three people took a petition with them," Amelia pointed out. "If they each get ten signatures, that's an extra thirty names!"

Sam broke into a smile. "Hey!" he said, pointing across the street. "Check it out."

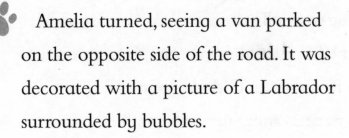

Amelia turned, seeing a van parked
on the opposite side of the road. It was
decorated with a picture of a Labrador
surrounded by bubbles.

"Aw, that's sweet!" Amelia peered at the
shop behind the van. A freshly painted
sign above the shop window read *Pooch
Parlour.* Her heart leapt. It was a new
dog-grooming business!

"Let's go in," said Amelia. "The owner
must love animals. They might sign our
petition."

Amelia stepped inside. The shop was
painted blue with black pawprints dotted
around the walls. A man with short black
hair was trimming the claws of a brown-

and-white Welsh sheepdog. He looked up and smiled. "Hello there, I'm Leon! Is this a new client?" He nodded at Mac, who cowered away.

"Poor Mac hates baths," Sam said, laughing as Mac whimpered and tried to duck behind his legs. "Don't worry, boy – I won't make you have a wash today!"

Amelia stepped in front of Mac and held out the petition. "We were just

wondering if you'd sign our petition?" she explained.

"Let's see ..." Leon put his clippers down and took the sheet of paper.

Mac crept forward and sniffed at the sheepdog. The sheepdog sniffed back. Then a cough from behind made Amelia turn. A woman in a sweater with curly, chin-length hair sat in an armchair in the corner of the shop, with a magazine open on her lap.

"Is this your dog?" asked Amelia. "He's beautiful!"

Mac yapped several times and the sheepdog gave a gruff woof. Amelia glanced over at them and laughed. They

were sniffing
each other
again, as if to
say, *Nice to
meet you!*

"Yes, that's
Solo," the woman said. "He's a working
sheepdog. I've just taken over a farm
near here. The farmer retired, you see."

"Is that Mr Nicholl's old farm?" Amelia
heart warmed, remembering the kindly
old man she and Sam had once met.

"That's the one! I'm Janie Dunn, by the
way." She tucked a brown curl behind
her ear.

"I'm Amelia, this is Sam and that . . ."

Amelia pointed at Mac, who was now running around Solo in a circle "… is Mac!"

Solo wore an amused expression. But despite Mac's yapping, he didn't seem keen to join the game of chase. "Solo's thirteen, so he's getting on a bit," Janie said. "He probably wishes he still had Mac's energy!"

The sheepdog gave a short growl

and bared his teeth at Mac. Amelia recognised it as a "that's enough" kind of growl.

"Come along!" Sam said, taking Mac's lead from his pocket and heading out the door. "Solo won't want to be your friend if you keep annoying him!"

"Done!" said Leon, clicking his pen shut. "Would you like to sign, Ms Dunn?"

Janie took the petition, signed it and handed it to Amelia. "I hope they take notice. We need to be encouraging wildlife, not building over it!"

"Exactly," said Amelia, nodding. "Thanks!"

"You're welcome. See you again soon!"

Janie replied, smiling.

"That's ten signatures now," Amelia
said to Sam, once they had left the shop.

"I bet we'll get loads more tomorrow
at the petting farm," said Sam.

Amelia nodded, feeling a swell of hope.
*Anyone who likes animals must see that this is
important!*

CHAPTER THREE

Saturday morning was warm and sunny. Amelia and Sam spotted lots of bees buzzing around the hedgerows as they walked up to the petting farm. Amelia was pleased to see that Caleb's parents had pinned up a copy of their petition by the entrance gate, so it was sure to be

seen by lots of visitors.

Caleb led them into the farmhouse kitchen, where a map of Welford was spread out on the table. "I was thinking we could start the trek by taking the llamas alongside these fields." He pressed his finger on a green square on the map marked *Welford Park*. "There's loads of nice grass for them to munch on."

"After that, we could trek along this

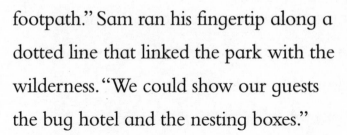

footpath." Sam ran his fingertip along a dotted line that linked the park with the wilderness. "We could show our guests the bug hotel and the nesting boxes."

"That's a brilliant idea!" said Amelia. "And if people actually see the wildlife, they'll understand why we need to save the sanctuary!"

A scream rang out suddenly, above the chatter of the visitors outside. Amelia jolted upright. "What was that?" She glanced over at the open window, just as another ear-piercing shriek sounded. She dashed out of the kitchen, followed by the two boys, and raced into the farmyard. Several children were clustered around the llama enclosure's fence and a small girl was sobbing, tears streaming down her face.

Amelia could hear growling and snorting. She rushed towards the enclosure and gasped in shock.

Llarry charged at Lliam. As Lliam ducked away, he caught Llarry's neck with his teeth. Llarry responded by whacking his neck against Lliam's side.

"The llamas are fighting!" wailed the little girl.

"I don't like it," whispered a little boy.

The children standing by the fence gaped at the spectacle. Llucinda, however, looked completely unimpressed as Lliam snorted and wrapped his long neck around Llarry's. She turned her back on the fighting llamas and picked at some grass instead.

"What are they doing?" said Sam, clutching Amelia's arm anxiously as Lliam dragged Llarry around in a circle, both necks still hooked together.

Amelia's fingers whitened as she gripped the fence. "They're neck-

wrestling. I read about it in a wildlife magazine. Some llamas do it for fun, but they can get badly hurt!"

"We need to stop them," Caleb said, his face pale. "But how?"

We have to break them apart – and quickly! Amelia looked around and caught sight of the hose that Mrs Parish used to fill the water troughs. "I know!" she cried out, running over to snatch it up.

"Good idea!" yelled Sam, sprinting to the tap and turning it. Water gushed out, and Amelia aimed the spray at the llamas. They broke apart, snorting indignantly.

"Well done!" Mrs Parish shouted as

she and her husband leapt over the gate.
They each grabbed a llama and pulled
them away from each other.

"This has never happened before."
Mr Parish frowned as he tied Llarry up.
"They've always got along really well!"

Sam turned the tap off. "At least
Llucinda isn't joining in," he pointed
out. "Maybe she'll calm the other two
down?"

As if deciding to prove Sam wrong, Llucinda flattened her ears back and snorted as a small girl reached over the fence and tried to stroke her. Llucinda jerked her chin up and spat. She missed the girl, but made her scream with shock.

"Oh no!" Mrs Parish quickly tied Lliam up and ran over to the girl and her parents. "I'm so sorry!"

This really isn't good for the petting farm, Amelia thought. She leaned in towards Sam. "We need to find a way to calm Llucinda down," she whispered.

"And we have to stop Lliam and Llarry fighting," he replied, "and sort out the llama drama!"

Later that afternoon, Amelia was
sprawled on the sofa in her living room,
researching llama facts on her tablet.
Sam had found a book about llamas
at the library, and was flicking through
the pages. Star, Amelia's kitten, leapt up
and curled herself into Amelia's lap as
she swiped through some websites. "Did
you know, a baby llama is called a cria?"
Amelia said.

"Nope!" Sam
laughed, turning
the page. "Did
you know that

llama dung is sometimes used as a fuel?"

"It says here that llamas are good at guarding sheep," said Amelia. She turned the tablet to show Sam a picture of a llama standing proudly beside a flock of sheep.

"This is interesting!" Sam tapped the book with his fingertip. "If you spoil llamas too much when they're young, they begin to think you're part of their herd. They can start spitting at you to keep you in your place and can be very difficult to handle."

Amelia sat bolt upright, and Star jumped off her lap. "That sounds like Llucinda!" she said. "Do you think her last family might have spoiled her?"

"But even if they did, that doesn't help us fix the problem," said Sam, frowning.

Amelia sighed. "And we still don't know why Lliam and Llarry are fighting." *How are we ever going to sort those llamas out?* she wondered.

CHAPTER FOUR

"Look at all those cars!" Amelia said, as Sam's dad drove them to the petting farm the next day. The road leading up to the farm's gate was lined with parked vehicles as far as she could see, and the driveway was packed too. *The village really does have a parking problem!*

"It's brilliant there are so many
visitors," said Sam. "It means the Parishes'
petting farm is successful!" Beside him,
Mac yapped, as if agreeing.

Sam's dad finally pulled into a space
alongside the kerb. "You won't forget
about taking the petition to the council
offices, will you?" Sam asked him.

"I'll drop it off on the way home,"
Sam's dad promised. "They'll be shut, but
I'll pop it through the letterbox."

Amelia and Sam got out of the car
and started walking up the road. It had
rained overnight, and they had to dodge
round several big muddy puddles. "I
can't believe we got nearly a hundred

signatures in just two days!" Amelia said. *The council can't ignore that many people*, she thought. *Can they?*

"It's brilliant!" Sam replied. "Hey, we'd better not be late for our very first llama tour!" They broke into a sprint and Mac dashed alongside them, easily keeping up despite his little legs.

But as they came out behind the goat pen, they heard loud snorts. Amelia ran towards the llama enclosure, just in time to see Lliam ram into Llarry's side. Llarry turned and snapped back at him with a whinny.

"Come on, Llucinda!" Mrs Parish said, sounding exasperated. She held a

halter up, but as she brought it close to Llucinda's nose, the llama ducked down. Mrs Parish tried again and again, but Llucinda just squirmed away each time. Eventually she swiped at Mrs Parish with her neck, nearly knocking her to the muddy ground.

She's trying to neck-wrestle with Mrs Parish — she really does think the Parishes are part of her herd! Amelia caught Sam's eye and he grimaced.

"Maybe a walk in the countryside will calm them down," Sam suggested.

Caleb distracted Llucinda with a stick of celery and his mother finally managed to slip the harness over her nose.

Sam waved Caleb over. "We had an idea for the tour," he told him. "As we're going through the wilderness, we  could tell people about the wildlife there."

"I designed a leaflet on Mum's computer," Amelia added, pulling some papers from her rucksack. "We can hand them out when we start the real tours."

"Great idea, guys!" Caleb took a leaflet and grinned as he read it. "Wow! I love your drawings!" He pointed to a picture of a woodpecker. Amelia felt her cheeks

warm – she was especially proud of that
one!

"I think we're ready!" Mrs Parish said,
handing Llucinda's lead to Caleb. "Sam
and Amelia, you can take Llarry and
Lliam. I was going to invite some friends
along, but what with the llamas being so
naughty, I think it's best if it's just us this
time. We can get them used to the route."

Lliam strolled happily alongside Amelia

as she led him out of the farmyard and on to the road, where sunshine reflected from the puddles. *We're trekking at last!* thought Amelia. She gripped Lliam's rope tightly, but he didn't seem to need much steering. She glanced back and saw Mrs Parish walking Mac on his lead, guiding the puppy away from something that had caught his eye in the hedge.

Thankfully, the trek seemed to settle

the llamas. They held their heads high, glancing about and enjoying the scenery. Llucinda strode out to the front, determined to lead the way, and Caleb had to walk extra fast to keep up. Amelia allowed herself to relax. *This is going really well!* She stroked Lliam on the neck to praise him.

As they walked, Mrs Parish told them facts about llamas. "They're used as pack animals in some countries," she explained. "But if you give them too much to carry, they'll just lie down and refuse to move!"

Amelia heard bleating and spotted sheep in the field beside them.

"Hey, there's Solo!"
Sam pointed to a
sheepdog lying in the
shade of a tree.

Amelia recognised
Janie Dunn's dog from
the grooming parlour. "I
expect he's working." She squinted to get
a better look and noticed that Solo was
panting heavily. "Oh dear, I don't think
he's enjoying the sunshine!"

"We should practise our speech for
the wilderness bit of the tour," said Sam.
"I reckon we should start with the bug
hotel. I can get people to look inside and
count the ladybirds and centipedes."

"Perfect!" Amelia said, excitedly. "And we can ask them if they can spot the chrysalis!"

Suddenly, Llarry snorted. Tossing his head up into the air, he yanked his lead out of Sam's hands and charged towards Lliam. Amelia was startled. She lost her grip on Lliam's lead and fell on to her bottom. Lliam whacked Llarry, who then lunged for Lliam's neck, trying to drag him to the ground. Llucinda snorted

and backed away from the male llamas, pulling Caleb with her.

Mrs Parish dashed forward and snatched hold of Sam and Amelia, tugging them back to a safe distance.

Lliam broke free from Llarry's hold, but Llarry aimed a kick at his side. Lliam shrieked, shying away, and then bolted towards the nearby field. He leapt over the fence, scattering the herd of terrified sheep.

Amelia's chest felt tight with worry. "We have to get Lliam back before he hurts himself or the sheep!"

"Or a human!" Sam added, his voice shaky.

"Go after him!" Mrs Parish urged Caleb. "I'll take care of Llarry and Llucinda!"

Caleb handed the leads to his mother and vaulted the fence. Sam unclipped Mac's lead, then he and Amelia jumped over the fence too. The three children ran into the middle of the field, followed by Mac who'd squeezed under the fence.

"Where did he go?" Caleb stopped suddenly and looked around.

"There!" yelled Sam, pointing across the field. Amelia caught sight of Lliam's tail disappearing through an open gate on the other side of the field, and she broke into a run again.

Solo sat up on his hind legs and barked
as they passed. He should have been
rounding up the sheep, who had fled
to the far corner of the field, but his
mouth hung open and his front legs were
shaking. Amelia's heart went out to him
– the old sheepdog didn't seem to have
the energy for herding. She couldn't stop
to cheer him up, though. There was a
llama on the loose!

They all ran into the woodland on
the other side of the gate and combed
through the trees and bushes, calling out
for Lliam.

Amelia's heart leapt as she saw a
flash of white fleece behind an elm tree.
"Lliam!" she cried, scrambling towards it.

But it was just a single sheep, separated

from the herd. There was no sign of
Lliam. Her heart thudded in her chest
as she turned to the two boys. Sam was
clutching his side, gasping for breath.

Caleb had sunk to his knees, panting.
He looked up at Amelia and Sam, and
his eyes were watery. "We've lost him,
haven't we?"

CHAPTER FIVE

"We can't give up!" Amelia clenched her fists in determination. "He must be nearby!"

"Let's search the village," Sam suggested.

The three children and Mac ran on to a muddy path that led through the woodland, straight to the main road. They peered into gardens, checked the grass verge for hoof prints and asked everyone they met if they'd seen a llama.

"If anything's happened to Lliam, it's my fault," Caleb said shakily. "It was my idea to do the trek."

"Don't blame yourself," said Amelia, as they passed the B&B.

"Amelia's right," said Sam. "You weren't to know … Oof!" Mac darted under Sam's feet, tripping him. The little dog barked loudly and leapt towards the gate.

68

"Oh, Mac, I know you're tired, but we've got to keep looking for Lliam!"

"We can't stop until we find him," said Caleb as Mac continued to yap and paw at the gate.

"What's wrong, boy?" Sam asked. He opened the gate, and Mac shot down the passage at the side of the house. Sam followed, then gasped. "Oh!"

He froze and Amelia almost walked right into him. She looked over Sam's shoulder.

The washing line had been tugged down, along with all

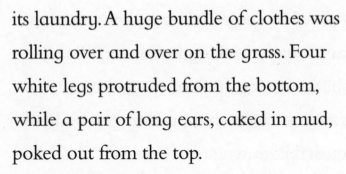

its laundry. A huge bundle of clothes was rolling over and over on the grass. Four white legs protruded from the bottom, while a pair of long ears, caked in mud, poked out from the top.

"Lliam!" all three children shouted at once.

Mac woofed.

"That's why you wanted us to stop here!" Sam ruffled Mac's head. "You sniffed him out. That definitely deserves a treat!"

Lliam stopped rolling around and let out a happy-sounding grunt.

"We need to get him out of that washing!" Amelia whispered as she tiptoed towards the llama, not wanting to startle him. "Playtime's over, Lliam," she said softly, peeling a pyjama top, emblazoned with a picture of a winged motorbike, away from his neck.

Lliam rested his head on Amelia's shoulder as she took more clothes off him. His shaggy coat was muddy-brown and heavy from the water it had soaked up. "Have you been rolling in a ditch?" Amelia stroked his neck gently with one hand, taking his lead with the other.

"Oh no – he's bleeding!" Caleb pulled a blood-stained pillowcase away from one of Lliam's back legs, revealing a deep scratch near the hoof.

"That looks really nasty," Sam said, crouching down to peer at the wound. "How did it happen?"

"He must have cut himself when he

jumped over the fence," Amelia said, wincing. "We need to get that looked at as soon as possible!"

"Oi!"

A man with a

shiny bald head and a beard leaned out of an upstairs window, clenching his fist. Amelia recognised him as Mr Ferguson, one of the regular B&B guests.

"Those are my favourite pyjamas!" Mr Ferguson pointed at the soggy trousers on the grass. "They're covered in mud!"

"I'm sorry!" Sam said hastily. "I'll make sure they get washed again."

Mr Ferguson huffed and slammed the window shut.

"We really need to take Lliam to Animal Ark," said Amelia, looking anxiously at the wound. "If that gets infected, he could be in serious trouble!"

"I'll ask Mum to phone your parents,

73

to let them know we've found Lliam,"
Sam said to Caleb. He bit his lip. "And
I'd better warn her about the washing
too …"

They called ahead to Animal Ark and
Mr Hope came out to meet them on the
surgery driveway. "I don't think we'll get
Lliam through the door!" he said. "Best
look at this leg right away."

Mrs Hope joined them on the

driveway with her treatment bag.

Lliam flinched as Mrs Hope started to clean the wound. Amelia stroked his neck. "I know it must hurt," she said gently. "But it won't take long, and then we can get you back home."

A small boy dragged his mother over to the surgery driveway and pointed. A pair of elderly ladies stopped behind them, then one pulled out a phone and took a photo.

"The wound's not too serious," Mrs Hope told Caleb. "Keep an eye on it, though, and bring him back if it doesn't heal."

"So why did Lliam run away?" Mr

Hope asked, frowning.

"He and Llarry have been up to all kinds of mischief lately," Amelia explained. "Ever since Llucinda arrived, they've been at each other's throats!"

"Literally," said Caleb gloomily.

"Ah, that explains it!" said Mr Hope, nodding. "I expect the two male llamas both want to get Llucinda's attention. They're jealous of each other, so they're fighting to impress her and get rid of the competition!"

"They'll stop eventually, though, won't they?" Caleb said, his forehead creasing.

"It's hard to say," Mr Hope admitted. "They might settle down over time.

Don't get your hopes up, though."

As they walked Lliam back along the High Street, plenty of people stopped to stare. Amelia noticed how calm the llama seemed though. *It must be because Llucinda's not around,* she realised.

"How are we going to clean him up?" Caleb wondered aloud. "It's not like he'll fit in the bathtub!"

"I know!" said Amelia, pointing at the dog-grooming parlour. "Maybe Leon can help."

She popped her head through the door of the Pooch Parlour. "Hello, Leon! We've got a new client for you!"

Leon gaped as he took in the muddy

llama standing on the pavement. He flashed a grin and grabbed the keys to his mobile grooming van. "I'll get him clean in no time!"

Mac backed away, whimpering, as Leon came out. The dog groomer pulled a hose from the van and aimed it at Lliam. To Amelia's surprise, the llama peeled back his lips in a grin as the spray hit his wool coat. A small crowd gathered on the pavement to watch.

"Here, rub some of this in!" Leon handed a bottle of shampoo to Amelia. She worked it through Lliam's coat. Once the llama was fully lathered up, Sam and Caleb took it in turns to rinse off the shampoo.

"Oh no!" said Caleb, suddenly. "I've just realised that I don't have any money with me. I'll call my parents and see if one of them can come over."

Leon laughed. "Don't be silly. With all this free publicity, I should be paying you!"

Mac gave a little yelp and leapt away from the soapy water running down Lliam's legs.

Afterwards, they dried Lliam off, patting him down with fluffy towels.

"The other llamas are going to be so jealous when they see you," Amelia said. "They're all going to want showers!"

"Oh dear," sighed Sam. "Mr Hope said Lliam and Llarry are already jealous of each other. If Llarry thinks Lliam's had special attention, he could get even worse!"

CHAPTER SIX

"Dad's giving us a lift to the petting farm," Sam said, as he crouched down to tie up his trainers in the B&B reception area.

It was the following Saturday, and Amelia had just arrived at Sam's house. "I hope the llamas have settled down

now," she said. "Hey, look what Dad sent me."

She passed Sam a postcard with a photo of a wolf lying on a rock. Its nose was pricked up as if it smelled something. "They live in the mountains in Italy," she said. "Wouldn't it be cool to see one in the wild?"

Just then, heavy boots stomped down the stairs and Mr Ferguson appeared, his face red and shiny. He snatched his leather jacket from the peg.

"Are you OK?" asked Amelia, putting her postcard away.

"Hmph!" grunted Mr Ferguson. He put his jacket on and zipped it up. "Some

stupid petition got sent to the council office. They gave me the job of turning a useless bit of wasteland into a car park – which, I might add," he wagged a finger at them both, "this village desperately needs. But apparently some people don't think we need a car park at all!"

He dug a set of keys out of his pocket. "Just as well I've already got the council's approval. So now I'm off for a nice, long motorbike ride. I need to relax after all that nonsense!" He stormed out, slamming the door behind him.

Amelia looked at Sam. His mouth hung wide open. "I knew Mr Ferguson sometimes did work for the council,"

he said. "But I never guessed he was in charge of building that car park! What are we going to do now?"

Amelia stared through the car window as Sam's dad drove them to the petting farm, barely noticing the view outside. She blinked back a tear. *Our petition was a waste of time!*

"There's the Hopes' car!" Sam said, interrupting her gloomy thoughts as his dad turned into the farmhouse driveway. "I wonder what they're here for?"

I hope none of the animals are poorly! thought Amelia.

At the llama enclosure, they found Mr Hope peering inside Llarry's mouth.

Mrs Hope
was trying
to persuade
Lliam to open
his firmly
clenched jaws.
Caleb stood

next to his father, chewing on his nails.

"What's going on?" asked Sam.

"Llarry and Lliam keep biting each
other," Mr Parish explained, with a
weary sigh. "The Hopes are trimming
their teeth so they don't cause any
damage." He pushed a hand through his
hair. "I don't understand it. They used to
get along together so well!"

Amelia tipped her head to one side, thinking hard. "Have you thought about separating them?"

Caleb nodded. "We tried that, but they kept jumping over the fence to be near Llucinda." He nodded toward the female. "She's not eating properly, either. I don't think she's happy here."

Oh dear, thought Amelia. *We've got to find a way to sort out this llama drama . . .*

Later that day, Amelia and Sam headed up to Animal Ark to check on some of the sick animals that had stayed at the surgery overnight.

"Everything's going wrong," Amelia sighed, feeding slices of carrot to a guinea pig. She couldn't even smile at the fluffy little creature, her heart felt so heavy. "The wilderness is getting concreted over and the llamas are miserable."

Sam stroked a sleepy rabbit who was

recovering from an anaesthetic. His eyebrows knotted in frustration. "I just can't think of a solution."

"There must be a way!" Amelia said, more confidently than she felt.

The door opened and Mrs Hope looked into the room. "We've got a Ms Dunn here with her sheepdog. Would you like to help?"

Amelia remembered the name and jumped up. "That must be Solo!"

She put the guinea pig back into its hutch. Sam carefully placed the sleeping rabbit in its basket and they both followed Mrs Hope through to the examination room.

Amelia knelt
to stroke the old
sheepdog. "How are
you doing, Solo?"

"He's not great,"
Janie Dunn replied,
sadly. "He's walking as though his legs
are made of lead! He used to be such a
live wire, too."

Mrs Hope tested each of Solo's legs,
one by one, gently moving them back
and forward, feeling the joints. "I'm
sorry to say he's got arthritis," she said,
eventually. "It's common in dogs his age.
I'll give you some supplement pills to mix
in with his food."

"I was afraid of that." Janie looked away and blinked fast. "Maybe it's time for him to retire. I'm sure I can find another dog to help with the sheep."

Poor Solo, Amelia thought. *I wonder how he'll feel about another dog taking his place?*

"Wait!" she cried, as an idea sprang into her mind. "Don't get a dog – get a llama!"

"What do you mean, Amelia?" asked Mrs Hope, raising her eyebrows.

"I read about it online when we were researching llamas," Amelia said. "They're easy to train and they make great guard animals for sheep!"

Sam nodded excitedly. "That's right …

and – oh!" His eyes lit up and he grinned at Amelia. "We just happen to know a llama who might need a new home …"

CHAPTER SEVEN

"It's a brilliant idea!" Mrs Parish clapped her hands as Amelia explained her plan for Llucinda in the farmhouse kitchen that evening. "She'll love being the only llama in the household. And Llarry and Lliam will settle down again if she's not around."

Amelia's heart swelled as she tucked into her curry. *We've finally found a way to make the llamas happy!*

"We'll still be able to visit Llucinda," Caleb said. "So it's all worked out in the end. Although…" He put his fork down, his smile fading. "I'm still really worried about Lliam running off again. Maybe we should just forget the whole llama trekking idea."

Amelia glanced over at Sam. He was chewing thoughtfully and staring out the kitchen window. "Maybe it wasn't a complete waste of time," he said slowly. "In fact, I think I've had an idea."

"What is it?" Caleb's eyes widened.

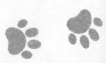

Sam leaned in towards Amelia and
Caleb, a grin spreading across his face …

The following morning, Amelia and
Sam sat on a bench by the village pond,
watching Mac sniff at the water's edge.
Amelia giggled as
a dragonfly zipped
past Mac's nose
and he jumped
back, startled.

Feeling a nudge
from Sam, she
glanced up. Mr Ferguson was strolling
towards the other side of the pond, one

hand in his pocket, the other clutching a paper bag. They were hidden by the tall reeds that lined the pond, so he hadn't spotted them yet.

"He always comes here when he visits Welford," Sam said with a grin. "Every Sunday, like clockwork. He's always in a good mood after one of Dad's fry-ups. Watch, he'll start feeding the ducks in a minute …"

Sure enough, Mr Ferguson opened the bag and scattered seed over the ground

in front of him. A look of contentment settled over his face as the ducks flapped out of the water and pecked around his feet.

"Are you ready?" Amelia whispered. She raised her eyebrows at Sam and he nodded back.

They stood up and walked towards Mr Ferguson. As they drew close, he quickly shoved the bag into his pocket. "Oh, hello, you two. I'm, um, just getting some fresh air. Nice day, isn't it?"

Why doesn't he want anyone to know he likes animals? Amelia wondered.

"We're just going for a walk," she said. "Do you want to join us? We can show

you some cool places in the village."

"Unless you'd rather stay here and feed the ducks?" Sam added.

"The ducks? No, no, no!" Mr Ferguson's face reddened all over. "Annoying creatures, really!" He patted his belly. "I suppose I could do with walking off my breakfast."

"Great, let's go this way!" Amelia started towards the wilderness.

They led Mr Ferguson along the footpath until they reached a rotting tree stump that marked the start of the wildlife sanctuary. A pair of stag beetles scurried in between its mossy roots.

"This is where our walking tour of the

wilderness begins!" said Amelia with a sweep of her hand.

"There are lots of cool creatures to see!" added Sam.

Mr Ferguson pursed his lips. "Last time I was here, this place looked like a rubbish dump."

"A lot has changed," said Sam. "We cleaned it up with some friends."

"This tells you all about the animals

that live in the sanctuary," said Amelia quickly. She handed Mr Ferguson one of the leaflets she had made for the llama trek. He peered at it and his eyes widened.

"We'll start with the bug hotel," Sam said, heading towards a wooden

box fixed to a branch. "Can you see the ladybirds? And I think a caterpillar has started weaving a chrysalis. That sign," he pointed

to a wooden sign hanging on the branch below, "tells you which insects are living there. You can try to spot them all if you like."

"If you see anything new, we'll add it to the sign," Amelia added.

Mr Ferguson stared at the bug hotel. "That's actually quite interesting," he muttered.

"This way," Amelia said, making her way towards a nest. "The woodpecker's over here, where the hammering sound is coming from!"

Mr Ferguson peered through the trees. "Oh! I think I can see it!" he cried out, pointing upwards at a flash of red.

The three of them stood back to
let a trio of runners pass them on the
path. Mac scampered over to a couple
picnicking on a fallen tree trunk.

"Leave them alone, Mac!" Sam called
out. "You've had your breakfast!"

The couple laughed and threw Mac a
bit of sausage, which he snaffled up.

"See? Everyone loves it here," Amelia
said softly, watching a smile curl on Mr
Ferguson's lips.

Mac started bounding back towards Sam, but he got distracted by a squirrel and chased it through the undergrowth. The squirrel escaped up a tree, but Mac kept on running around looking for it. Mr Ferguson burst into laughter, quickly pressing a hand against his mouth and disguising it as a cough.

They led him around the rest of the wilderness, showing him a badger track, the wild flowers and some other nests. Soon he was smiling, but a little sadly.

"We hope you've enjoyed your tour today," Sam said. "Every time we come here there are new creatures to discover."

Mr Ferguson held his hands up in

surrender. "All right, I get it! You really want to save this place." His eyebrows folded in a deep frown. "Was it you two who started the petition?"

Amelia and Sam nodded.

"Please, Mr Ferguson, don't build the car park," pleaded Amelia. "You can see how many creatures have made their homes here. Don't take that away from them!"

"But it's the perfect place," Mr Ferguson insisted, sighing.

"Think of the woodpeckers," Sam urged him. "They can't live in a car park!"

"I do see your point, it's just …" Mr

Ferguson took a hanky from his pocket and wiped it across his forehead.

"There's the squirrels and caterpillars and ladybirds, too," Amelia said, her heart beating fast. "They'll all have to find somewhere else to live."

Mr Ferguson nodded, gazing around. "I like what you've done here," he said. "I can see it's good for the community." He shook his head. "But there's a real problem with parking in Welford. If we don't build a car park here, where can we build one?"

"Funny you should ask that!" Amelia said. She flashed a grin at Sam, her heart galloping. "We have an idea!"

CHAPTER EIGHT

Sam led Mr Ferguson across the road and pointed to an empty field at the edge of the petting farm. "What about building the car park there? We already asked the Parishes and they don't mind."

"They said they don't use that field, so it might as well be used for parking,"

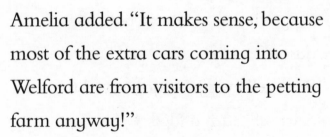

Amelia added. "It makes sense, because most of the extra cars coming into Welford are from visitors to the petting farm anyway!"

Mr Ferguson stared at the field, muttering under his breath. He looked up and down it, as if measuring it with his eyes.

Amelia held her breath. *Please say yes!*

Mr Ferguson nodded briefly. "All right. I can't make any promises, but I think I can persuade the council it'll work." He bent down to stroke Mac's ears, giving a little snort as the little Westie pawed his beard.

Amelia let out all the air in her lungs

in a big whoosh. "Thank you, Mr
Ferguson!"

"We'll tell everyone you saved the
wilderness!" Sam added.

Amelia felt giddy as she high-fived
Sam. *We did it!*

Two Sundays later, an excited Caleb
led Amelia and Sam back to the field,
which was full of workers now. Nearby,
a woman was peering through a camera
on a tripod, her back pressed up against
the fence. A little further off, a workman
was driving a digger back and forth
across the field.

"He's flattening the earth so the
tarmac can go on top," Caleb explained.

Amelia felt a little sad that the grass
in the field would be lost. *But at least the
wilderness is safe – lots of animals can make
their homes there instead!*

"Is that Mr Ferguson?" Sam pointed at
a man standing with his back to them,
holding up a clipboard and wearing a

bright yellow safety vest. He turned and, catching sight of the children, waved.

They all waved back.

"Mum never did get the llama toe prints out of his favourite pyjamas," Sam whispered. "But he still came back to stay, so I think he's forgiven us!"

Hearing grunts behind her, Amelia turned. Mrs Parish was walking towards them, leading Llarry and Lliam on either side of her.

"Hello!" Amelia said, reaching out to stroke Lliam. "Don't even think about jumping over this fence!"

"Hey!" a voice called out, and Amelia saw the surveyor pat her coat pocket and

point at Llarry. A sandwich bag was hanging from his mouth. "That's my lunch!"

"Llarry!" Mrs Parish looked mortified. She tugged the bag from the llama's jaws and handed it back to the surveyor.

"Sorry!" Caleb said to the surveyor, and he led Llarry back from the fence.

"They're still being mischievous then?" asked Amelia, laughing.

"Definitely!" Mrs Parish replied. "But

they're nowhere near as bad as before. They're best friends again, now that it's just the two of them."

"Three's a crowd, eh, Lliam?" Sam said, patting him.

"Thank you, Sam and Amelia, for everything you've done," Mrs Parish said with a warm smile. "You've solved the parking problem, and you sorted out our llama drama! We've got the tours up and running now. In fact, I need to get back and start one now. They're a big hit!"

Sam looked at his watch. "We need to head off too," he said. "Mum's cooking lunch."

Amelia ran her fingers through Lliam's

thick coat. "Bye, Lliam."

"Try not to get into any more trouble," Sam said, patting Llarry's neck.

They left Caleb and his mother leading the llamas back to their enclosure and headed out of the farm, saying goodbye to the other animals as they went.

Passing Janie Dunn's farmhouse, they saw her pulling her wellies off outside the front door. She waved to them.

"Want to come in and see how Llucinda is getting on?" called Janie.

"Yes, please," replied Amelia and Sam.

As Janie led them in through the lounge, Solo looked up from a basket in the corner and barked. Amelia ruffled the fur on his head and he licked her hand. "Happy retirement, Solo," she said, before following the others through the house and out into the field.

The main herd of sheep was gathered in the near corner, but

Llucinda was nowhere nearby.

"There she is!" said Sam suddenly.
He pointed at the far corner, where the
brown llama was chivvying a few sheep
back towards the herd.

"Llucinda is an excellent guard llama!"
Janie said. "The sheep don't seem to
mind her bossing them about. She
definitely likes being the one in charge!"

"Thanks for taking her, Janie," Amelia
said.

"I should be thanking you!" Janie
replied. "I'd never have thought about
getting a llama to mind the sheep if it
wasn't for you two!"

As Llucinda urged the three sheep

back to the main herd, a fat lamb bolted away, stumbling on some uneven ground. Llucinda ran over and nosed it towards its mother. She ran in a circle around the herd in her funny bouncing gait.

Amelia and Sam laughed. Llucinda's ears swivelled at the sound and she ran towards them.

"Hello, Llucinda," Amelia said, stroking the llama's neck.

Llucinda made a soft humming sound and a warmth spread through Amelia's chest. *We really did find a way to make her happy!*

She and Sam waved at Janie and Solo as they left the farmhouse and hurried back to the B&B.

"I can't wait to get back to Animal Ark tomorrow," Sam said. "I wonder what animals are waiting for us there."

"Mrs Hope said a whole family of ferrets have an appointment tomorrow," Amelia said.

"Ferrets sound like fun!" Sam grinned. "But I've heard they can be quite a handful."

"Nothing we can't handle," Amelia said, smiling back.

The End

Read on for a sneak peek at
Amelia and Sam's next adventure!

ANIMAL ARK

Bumper special with two stories!

Reindeer Recovery

Lucy Daniels

"Look at this!" Amelia said, holding up a tiny golden reindeer for Sam to see. She turned it in her hand, making it sparkle under the bright lights of the treatment room at Animal Ark. "It's one of Father Christmas's reindeer!"

Amelia hung the decoration on the little Christmas tree beside Mr Hope's desk, nestling it between a shiny red bauble and a shimmering icicle.

Sam delved into the cardboard box on the treatment table, making the paper inside rustle. "Here's another one!" he said, drawing out a reindeer covered in red glitter. He hooked it on to a low branch beside a silver star.

"You two are doing a fantastic job," Mr Hope said, coming back into the room with an armful of tinsel. "I'm really starting to feel Christmassy now! Are you all ready for the Extravaganza next Sunday?"

Amelia grinned and nodded. "My costume's nearly done!" she said. "Mrs Cranbourne's just making the final adjustments."

"We're both going to be elves in the parade," Sam said. "We get to throw sweets into the crowd."

Amelia felt a thrill of excitement as she thought of the Extravaganza. The school choir was going be there, along with most of her class. *I can't wait!*

"Caleb and Izzy are dressing up too," Sam told Mr Hope. "They're in charge of collecting donations. All the money is going to a guide dog charity, so we're hoping to make as much as possible."

Mr Hope smiled. "Well, if you put as much energy into the parade as you do into helping at the surgery, it's bound to be a big success. Do you know who's going to play Father Christmas?" he asked. Then, tucking his thumbs into imaginary braces, he let out a deep "Ho, ho, ho!"

Amelia giggled. With his short brown

hair and dark-rimmed spectacles, Mr
Hope couldn't have looked less like
Father Christmas. "No one's told us
who's playing Santa yet," she said.

Sam frowned slightly. "It's funny we
don't know – we're going to be his elves,
after all!"

Mr Hope glanced up at the clock.
"Well, maybe I can help you there. Mrs
Cranbourne and Miss Fizz are due for
an appointment shortly. You can ask Mrs
Cranbourne then – she must know, since
she's the one organising everything." The
intercom on Mr Hope's desk bleeped.
"That will be her now!" he said, picking
up the receiver. "Send her through," Mr

Hope told Julia, the receptionist.

The door to the treatment room opened, and Mrs Cranbourne came in holding an animal carrier. The look of worry on the elderly lady's face sent a jolt of alarm through Amelia.

Read Reindeer Recovery
to find out what happens next...

Animal Advice

Do you love animals as much as Amelia and

Sam? Here are some tips on how to look after

them from veterinary surgeon Sarah McGurk.

Caring for your pet

1   Animals need clean water at all times.

2   They need to be fed too – ask your vet what kind of

food is best, and how much the animal needs.

3   Some animals, such as dogs, need exercise every day.

4   Animals also need lots of love. You should always

be very gentle with your pets and be careful not to do

anything that might hurt them.

When to go to the vet

Sometimes animals get ill. Like you, they will mostly get better on their own. But if your pet has hurt itself or seems very unwell, then a trip to the vet might be needed. Some pets also need to be vaccinated, to prevent them from getting dangerous diseases. Your vet can tell you what your pet needs.

Helping wildlife

1   Always ask an adult before you go near any animals you don't know.

2   If you find an animal or bird which is injured or can't move, it is best not to touch it.

3   If you are worried, you can phone an animal charity such as the RSPCA (SSPCA in Scotland) for help.

Where animals need you!

Kitten Rescue
Lucy Daniels

Bunny Trouble
Lucy Daniels

Fox Cub Danger
Lucy Daniels

Puppy in Peril
Lucy Daniels

The Purrfect Sleepover
Lucy Daniels

Doggy Drama
Lucy Daniels

Runaway Hamster
Lucy Daniels

Guinea Pig Superstar
Lucy Daniels

The Lonely Pony
Lucy Daniels

Scaredy-Dog
Lucy Daniels

Lost Kitten
Lucy Daniels

Llama on the Loose
Lucy Daniels

www.animalark.co.uk